For Belle and Kitty, and for all good partners. —B.R.W.

Text copyright © 1999 by Betty Ren Wright.
Illustrations copyright © 1999 by Kevin O'Malley.

Published by BridgeWater Paperback, an imprint and trademark of Troll Communications L.L.C.

Published in hardcover by BridgeWater Books.

Printed in the United States of America.

10 9 8 7 6 5 4 3 2 1

Library of Congress Cataloging-in-Publication Data

Wright, Betty Ren.
Pet detectives / by Betty Ren Wright; illustrated by Kevin O'Malley.
p.   cm.
Summary: Policeman Jack's dog Belle and cat Kitty do their bit to fight crime
on a daily basis and combine forces to capture a burglar.
ISBN 0-8167-4952-3 (lib. bdg.)   ISBN 0-8167-5652-X (pbk.)
[1. Dogs—Fiction. 2. Cats—Fiction. 3. Robbers and outlaws—Fiction. 4. Stories in rhyme.]
I. O'Malley, Kevin, ill. II. Title.
PZ8.3.W93Pe 1999
[E]—dc21   98-31228

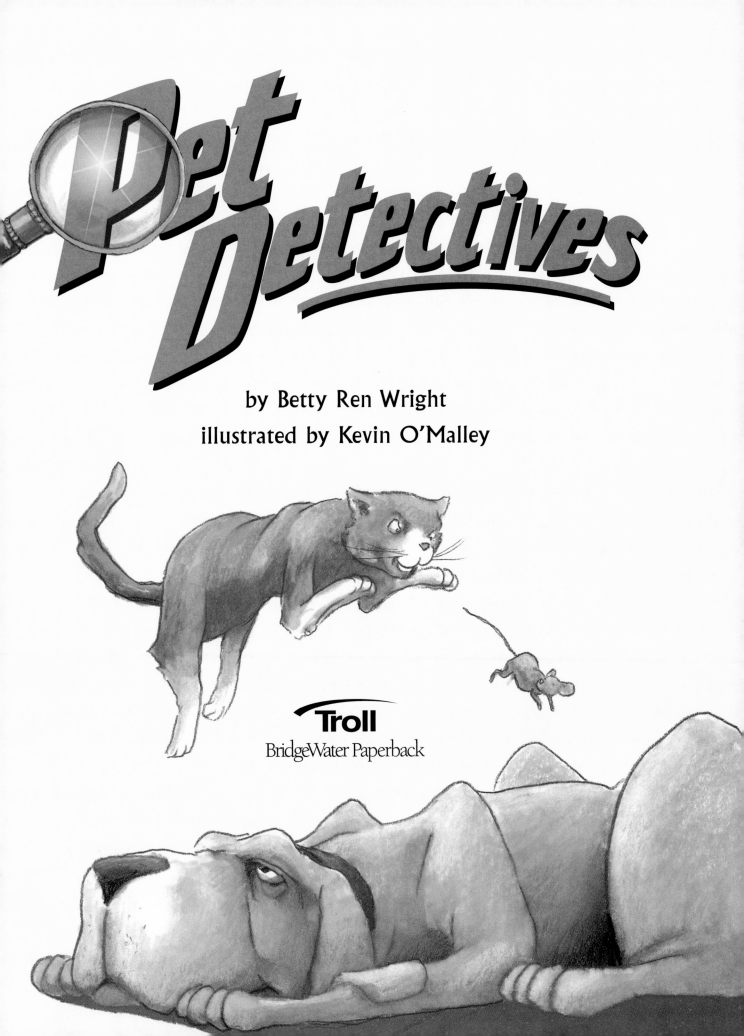

Pet Detectives

by Betty Ren Wright

illustrated by Kevin O'Malley

Troll
BridgeWater Paperback

Every day when the sun came up,
Policeman Jack fed his cat and pup,
drank some juice,
ate Krispy Krunch,
and packed a ham-on-rye for lunch.

Then, with pats for Belle and Kitty,
off he went to guard the city,

and all through the years he never knew
that Belle and Kitty were policemen, too.

Each day when Jack drove down the hill,
leaving the house locked up and still,
Police-cat Kitty went on patrol.
He tracked down every mouse who stole
crackers and cheese
or tried to munch
Policeman Jack's own Krispy Krunch.

"I'm great!" he said. "A hero! A whiz!
Without a doubt, the best there is!"

HE WAS ONE PROUD CAT.

Police-dog Belle didn't work as hard.
If she heard a footstep in the yard,
she yawned, then stretched, and stood with a sigh.
She didn't care who was passing by.
"Ho-hum," she said. "I'd rather sleep."

But her teeth were huge and her snarl was deep.
And she made such horrible monster faces
that visitors ran for safer places.

People with packages, people with mail,
people with magazines for sale—
with a terrified gasp or a panicked yell,
all of them ran from Police-dog Belle.

"Oh, yes," said Belle. "I'm strong! A whiz!
Absolutely the best there is!"

"NOT REALLY!"
GRUMPED KITTY.

Once, Kitty tried to find a way
to keep his friend awake all day
('cause working alone can be rather boring,
especially when your partner's snoring).
He rattled the doorknobs and broke a cup.
Belle just yawned and didn't look up.

He rolled a ball across her toes
and sprinkled catnip on her nose.
He burst a balloon right near her ear
and sang as he swung from the chandelier.
"You're loud," Belle growled, "and quite a clown,
but I do my police work lying down."

"I GIVE UP!"
GROANED KITTY.

Kitty continued to search the house,
arresting flies and nabbing a mouse,
but the days were long, 'cause Policeman Jack
was working overtime trying to track
a daring thief who every day
broke into a house—and got away!

One morning, when Kitty was up on a shelf,
chasing and capturing all by himself,
and Belle was asleep on the pantry floor,
there came a sound at the kitchen door.

CLICK . . .

SOMEONE WAS

PICKING

THE LOCK!

"Meeeooow!" cried Kitty. He flicked his tail,
flattened his ears, gave a terrified wail,
and hissed at Belle, "This burglar's real!
Wake up! Wake up! He's come to steal!"
But Belle dozed on as the door swung wide
and the wily burglar stepped inside.

**"IF I WEREN'T
A POLICE-CAT,"
KITTY SAID,
"I'D FAINT!"**

Then he hurtled down from that cupboard shelf,
with a screech so loud he scared himself.
He sailed like a comet through the air
and buried his claws in the burglar's hair.
The startled thief gave a mighty roar—
"My head's on fire!"—then fell to the floor.

At that, Belle opened one sleepy eye
and looked around with a lazy sigh.

She saw . . . A BURGLAR STRETCHED OUT FLAT,
WEARING A MOST PECULIAR HAT:
It had four cat feet and a scared cat face
and a cat tail whipping all over the place.

"What's this?" Belle barked. She forgot her nap.
In a flash, in the blink of an eye, in a snap,
she leaped to her feet with a monstrous growl,
and that horrified thief began to howl.

POLICE-DOG BELLE
WAS ON THE CASE!

Then out the door and across the yard
the burglar scrambled, breathing hard.
His coat was torn, his pants were ripped,
he shook his head (which Kitty still gripped).

He stumbled once, dropped to his knees,
and shouted, "Won't somebody help me, PLEASE!"

Now, wasn't it lucky what happened then?
Policeman Jack came home again!

That night on the news, the mayor of the city
had scrumptious rewards for Belle and Kitty.
He warned, "Beware of this cat and this pup.
If you see them coming, you'd better give up!"

Now Kitty is searching for mice once more,
and Belle lies sleeping near the door.
One is a worker,
one likes to dream,
but when there's trouble they're a fearless team.

"We're smart!" mews Kitty.
"We're brave!" barks Belle.
"Together we're doing very well.
This team is a marvel, a wonder, a whiz!
WE'RE ABSOLUTELY THE BEST THERE IS!"

AND THEY ARE!